OSTRICH
AND LARK

Marilyn Nelson

Illustrated by
San artists of the
Kuru Art Project
of Botswana

BOYDS MILLS PRESS
Honesdale, Pennsylvania

With loving gratitude to my friend Father Jacques de Foïard Brown,
who took me to visit a !Kung San village in the Kalahari Desert
so I would understand why we should try to do something to help them.
And deep thanks to Maude Brown of the Kuru Art Project.

—MN

The publisher wishes to thank Maude Brown of the Kuru Art Project for her work as interpreter and coordinator.
Without her thoughtful and generous help in communicating with the artists during the long process of creating
Ostrich and Lark, this book would not have been possible.

Boyds Mills Press, Inc.
815 Church Street
Honesdale, Pennsylvania 18431
Printed in China

ISBN: 978-1-59078-702-1
Library of Congress Control Number: 2011926647
First edition
The text of this book is set in Challoops.
The illustrations are done in oils on canvas.

10 9 8 7 6 5 4 3 2 1

A Note about the !Kung San

The !Kung San people are one of the many groups left of the people formerly known as the Bushmen of Southern Africa. They consider most of the names others call them, "Bushmen" included, insulting. They prefer to be called by their own group names: Jul'hoansi, !Kung, Naro, and llAnikhwe, among others. They live lightly on the earth, leaving almost no footprint. Their language is one with many click sounds.

Many of us have seen and heard N!xau, the delightful San actor, in the movie series *The Gods Must Be Crazy*. In reality, the lives of the San are extremely precarious. As farms and wild animal parks shrink their hunting lands, the San have been slowly displaced, their old way of life made impossible because of development. They live in what is mostly the Kalahari Desert and often are denied access to the water wells that exist on the land they once inhabited freely. They are hunter-gatherers forced to enter a twenty-first-century economic environment. Now their only means of survival is to learn how to make money.

The paintings for this book were created by San artists who are members of the Kuru Art Project of Botswana: Cgoma Simon, Gamnqoa Kukama, Jan Tcega, Qgõcgae Cao, Thamae Kaashe, Χgaoc'o Χare (Qhaqhoo). The author's proceeds from the sale of this book will be donated to the Kuru Art Project, part of a family of organizations dedicated to empowering the !Kung San with cultural revival and modern survival techniques, such as training programs in income-generation, leadership, and other skills. More information can be found at culturalsurvival.org/ourpublications/csq/article/the-kuru-family-organizations.

—MN

Ostrich and Lark started each morning together

at first light,
day in and day out.

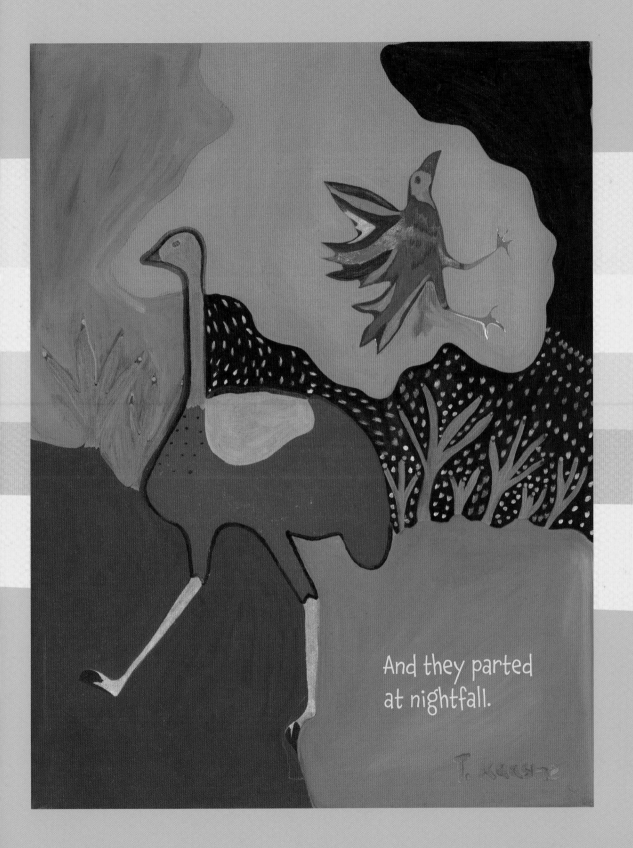

And they parted
at nightfall.

T. Karusa

Every day they nibbled an ongoing meal:

a few seeds here,

a few seeds there;

for Ostrich, the occasional lizard.

All day the sun glared out of cloudless blue.

Every day, all day,
over the cicada's drone,
a drizzle of buzzings fell,
and a downpour of birdsong.

Hornbill, Bee-eater, Hoopoe, Diederik,
Mousebird, Whydah, Canary:
from gray-light-come to last-light-gone,
the fancy-dressed suitors of the veld
warbled their rain-shower jazz.

But Ostrich was silent.

Lark sang the first song of the day,
perched tall, slender, and tawny brown
on a termite castle
or a low branch of a camel thorn tree.

But Ostrich was silent.

When Lark sang,
he flickered his wings,
and his white throat feathers trembled.
All day Lark sang, standing still or flitting,
his open wings vermillion-spangled.

But Ostrich was silent.

J. TCEGA

At dusk Lark sought his hidden nest on the ground.

Ostrich sat down
under an acacia tree
and tucked his head
under one of his black-and-white wings.

Sometimes he dreamed of flying.
Sometimes he dreamed of singing the sky full of stars.

Sometimes he dreamed
of the green season, drinking
caught water, and drinking, and drinking.

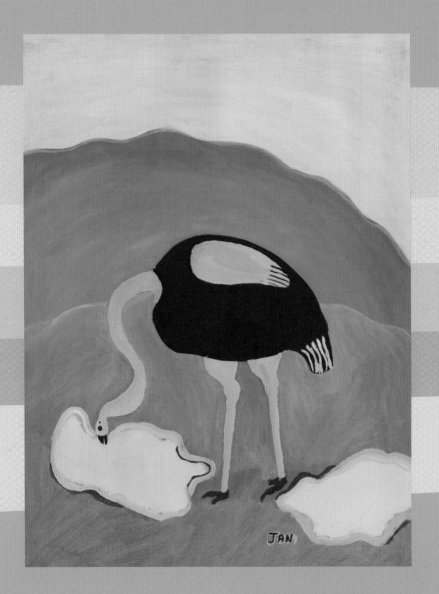

At first light, Lark called,
and together they started their day.

One evening,
as the great red sun
sank toward the tree-spiked horizon
and the birds swooped to their nests;

as the plant eaters gathered at full alert
and the meat eaters woke to prowl;
as the gates of night opened to the dark,

Ostrich fluttered his billowy wings.
He stretched his graceful neck,
closed his eyes, and

TWOO-WOO-WOOOT

Ostrich found his voice,
a voice part lion's roar,
part foghorn,
part old man trumpeting into his handkerchief.

Ostrich was booming!

Which is what ostriches do.

The veld fell silent.

And Ostrich boomed like thunderheads on the horizon. Ostrich boomed like the rainstorm that ends the dusty months of thirst.

GAMNOOA

Ostrich boomed like the promise
of jubilant green, like the promise of birth.

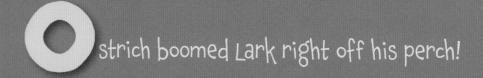 strich boomed Lark right off his perch!

Lark flew up to an
Ostrich-high branch
and looked at his friend
with a big WOW in his eyes.

GAMAQOA

Ostrich had found his voice at last,

his own beauty,
his big, terrific self.